MR.SILLY

by Roger Hargreaves

Mr Silly lives in Nonsenseland, which is a very funny place to live.

You see, in Nonsenseland, everything is as silly as can be.

In Nonsenseland the trees are pink!

And the grass is blue!

Isn't that silly?

In Nonsenseland dogs wear hats!

And do you know how birds fly in Nonsenseland?

No, they don't fly forwards.

They fly backwards!

It really is a very silly place indeed.

Which of course is why Mr Silly lives there.

Mr Silly, in fact, lives in quite the silliest-looking house you have ever seen in your whole life.

Have you ever seen a sillier looking house than that?

Now, this particular story is all about the Nonsense Cup.

You see, in Nonsenseland each year they hold a competition, and the Cup is awarded to whoever has the silliest idea of the year.

Mr Silly had never won the Cup, but each night, lying in his bed, he dreamed about winning it.

In order to win the Nonsense Cup Mr Silly realised that he would have to think up something remarkably silly.

He pondered over the problem one morning at breakfast.

Incidentally, you may be interested to know what Mr Silly was having for breakfast.

He was having a cup of coffee, which he put a spoonful of marmalade into.

After that he had a cornflake sandwich.

And to finish he had a boiled egg. But being Mr Silly, he ate the shell as well!

Isn't that a silly breakfast!

Anyway, this particular breakfast time, Mr Silly was thinking how to win that Cup.

He remembered two years ago the Cup was won by Mr Ridiculous.

He won by wallpapering his house.

Which sounds very ordinary, but in fact Mr Ridiculous had wallpapered the *outside* of his house!

And Mr Silly remembered last year when Mr Foolish won the Cup.

Mr Foolish, who was a friend of Mr Silly's, had won the Cup by inventing a car.

It was quite a normal car, apart from one thing. It had square wheels!

Isn't that silly?

Mr Silly thought and thought and thought, but it was no good.

He even had another cup of coffee with marmalade, but that didn't help either.

So, he decided to take a walk.

Off he went, leaving his front door open so that he wouldn't have burglars when he was out.

On his walk Mr Silly met a chicken wearing wellington boots and carrying an umbrella.

"Wouldn't it be silly if you didn't wear wellington boots and carry an umbrella?" he said to the chicken.

"Meow!" said the chicken, because animals in Nonsenseland don't make the same noises as they do in your country.

On his walk Mr Silly met a worm wearing a top hat, monocle and an old school tie.

"Wouldn't it be silly if you didn't wear a top hat, a monocle and an old school tie?" he said to the worm.

"Quack! Quack!" said the worm.

Next Mr Silly met a pig wearing trousers and a bowler hat.

"Wouldn't it be silly if you didn't wear trousers and a bowler hat?" he asked the pig.

"Moo!" said the pig.

Isn't that silly?

It was in the middle of Mr Silly's walk that he had his idea.

It was a beautifully silly idea.

Quite the silliest idea he'd ever had.

He hurried into town, and bought himself a pot of paint and a paintbrush.

The day of the great awarding of the Nonsense Cup arrived.

A huge crowd assembled in the City Square to see who was going to win the Cup.

The King of Nonsenseland mounted the specially built platform.

"Ladies and gentlemen," he said to the crowd in the City Square. "It is my pleasure today to award the Nonsense Cup to whoever has had the silliest idea of the year."

"One of the silliest ideas of the year," continued the King, "is by Mr Muddle the farmer. He has managed to grow, of all things, a square apple!"

The crowd clapped as the square apple was held up by Mr Muddle for everybody to see.

He felt sure he was going to win.

"However," said the King, and Mr Muddle's face fell, "we have had an even sillier idea entered by Mrs Nincompoop."

It was a teapot. Quite the silliest teapot there'd ever been.

The crowd broke into thunderous applause.

"I therefore have great pleasure," announced the King, "in presenting the Nonsense Cup to. . ."

Just then he looked up, and stopped in astonishment.

Now in the middle of the City Square there is a tree.

It's always been there, and it was at this tree that the King was looking in astonishment.

"What," he cried, "has happened to that tree?"

Everybody turned to look. The tree had green leaves!

Bright green leaves!

Not pink leaves like all the tree in Nonsenseland, but green.

There was an amazed silence.

"It was me," piped up Mr Silly. "I painted all the leaves green last night when you were all asleep!"

"A green tree!" exclaimed the King. "Whoever heard of a green tree?"

"A green tree!" shouted the crowd. "How silly!" And they started to applaud.

Mr Silly smiled modestly.

The King held up his hands.

"I think," he said, "that this is the silliest idea I have ever heard of, and therefore I award the Nonsense Cup to Mr Silly!"

The crowd cheered and cheered.

Mr Silly went pink with pride.

And a bird, perched high up in the branches of the silly green tree, looked down.

"Woof!" it said, and flew off, backwards!

Fantastic offers for Little Miss fans!

Collect all your Mr. Men or Little Miss books in these superb durable collectors' cases!
Only £5.99 inc. postage and packing, these wipe-clean, hard-wearing cases will give all your Mr. Men or Little Miss books a beautiful new home!

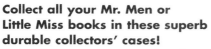

Keep track of your collection with this giant-sized double-sided Mr. Men and Little Miss Collectors' poster.
Collect 6 tokens and we will send you a brilliant giant-sized double-sided collectors' poster! Simply tape a £1 coin to cover postage and packaging in the space provided and fill out the form overleaf.

STICK £1 COIN HERE (for poster only)

Only need a few Little Miss or Mr. Men to complete your set? You can order any of the titles on the back of the books from our Mr. Men order line on 0870 787 1724. Orders should be delivered between 5 and 7 working days.

--- TO BE COMPLETED BY AN ADULT ---

To apply for any of these great offers, ask an adult to complete the details below and send this whole page with the appropriate payment and tokens, to: MR. MEN CLASSIC OFFER, PO BOX 715, HORSHAM RH12 5WG

☐ Please send me a giant-sized double-sided collectors' poster.
AND ☐ I enclose 6 tokens and have taped a £1 coin to the other side of this page.

☐ Please send me ☐ Mr. Men Library case(s) and/or ☐ Little Miss library case(s) at £5.99 each inc P&P

☐ I enclose a cheque/postal order payable to Egmont UK Limited for £...............................

OR ☐ Please debit my MasterCard / Visa / Maestro / Delta account (delete as appropriate) for £...............................

Card no. ☐☐☐☐☐☐☐☐☐☐☐☐☐☐☐☐☐☐☐☐☐☐☐☐   Security code ☐☐☐

Issue no. (if available) ☐☐   Start Date ☐☐/☐☐/☐☐   Expiry Date ☐☐/☐☐/☐☐

Fan's name: ....   Date of birth: ....

Address: ....

....

....   Postcode: ....

Name of parent / guardian: ....

Email for parent / guardian: ....

Signature of parent / guardian: ....

Please allow 28 days for delivery. Offer is only available while stocks last. We reserve the right to change the terms of this offer at any time and we offer a 14 day money back guarantee. This does not affect your statutory rights. Offers apply to UK only.

☐ We may occasionally wish to send you information about other Egmont children's books.
If you would rather we didn't, please tick this box.

Ref: LIM 001